ONLY BONES LEFT BEHIND

By
Tom Hamling

Illustrated By Rachel Edwards

This Book Belongs To

....

Titles available from Tom Hamling

For my kiddies...

...make the most of every adventure!

A special thank you to Becca,
Rae and Amy for all their support!

My name is Bella

How do you do?

I'm going on an adventure

Would you like to come too?

Today I am a ranger

In a Jurassic land

Jack is here with me

Holding my hand

He is a little scared

Of what we might find

"They are extinct" I explain

"Only bones left behind"

Jack looks puzzled

So I have to explain

"Dinosaurs lived here...

...but none remain"

"Dinosaurs?!" He gasps

His legs start to shake

"I was only scared

Of seeing a snake!"

We giggle together

And roll to the ground

But we quickly jump up

When we hear a sound

The noise gets closer

And louder than before

Lots of heavy footsteps

And then a fearsome roar!

Tiny arms, thick sharp claws

And wobbly knobbly knees

He slowly opens up his mouth

And whispers "Help me please"

He seems a friendly dinosaur

But with very scary teeth

Lifting up his spiky tail

He shows us underneath

A thorn is poking in his skin

He roared again and cried

"We need to pull it out Jack

But it's very deep inside"

We both take hold and slowly pull

With a squish the thorn flies out

The dinosaur claps and smiles

And then begins to shout

"Thank you, thank you, thank you

And thank you once again"

Jack feels brave and shouts straight back

"Dinosaur, what is your name?"

"I'm Roary" He says

With a big friendly grin

"I too have a sister

Come and meet my twin"

We follow through the trees

For what seems like forever

We are still a little scared

But at least we are together

"This is Whisper, my sister

She is friendly too

So, please don't be worried

She would never hurt you"

"These are my friends" said Roary

"They have just helped me!"

"I'm pleased to meet you

Will you join us for tea?"

We sit down to eat

Some branches and leaves

But we have to go soon

Back home through the trees

We say goodbye

And go home to our beds

We are very tired

So we rest our heads

In our pyjamas

Blankets up to our chins

Waiting for tomorrow

When a new adventure begins

THE END

Tom lives with his wife and two children in Norwich, UK.
He and his wife both write for popular parenting blog
'See What Mummy Says'.
Tom's first children's book 'It's Gold We Love Most!' was
launched in 2019.

The book is illustrated by Rachel Edwards.
Rachel graduated from Norwich University of the Arts
in 2017, and lives in Maidstone, UK.

"See what Mummy says..."

Follow Tom and his family's adventures here:

Website: www.seewhatmummysays.com
Twitter: @whatmummysaysuk
Instagram: seewhatmummysays
Facebook: See What Mummy Says

Printed in Poland
by Amazon Fulfillment
Poland Sp. z o.o., Wrocław